# MIGHTY MORPHIN POWER RANGERS

SABAN'S

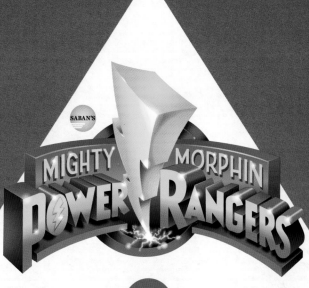

8

WRITTEN BY
**KYLE HIGGINS**
ILLUSTRATED BY
**HENDRY PRASETYA**

COLORS BY
**MATT HERMS**
LETTERS BY
**ED DUKESHIRE**

COVER BY
**JAMAL CAMPBELL**
DESIGNER
**JILLIAN CRAB**
ASSISTANT EDITOR
**MATTHEW LEVINE**
ASSOCIATE EDITOR
**ALEX GALER**
EDITOR
**DAFNA PLEBAN**

HASBRO SPECIAL THANKS
**BRIAN CASENTINI,**
**MELISSA FLORES,**
**EDGAR PASTEN,**
**PAUL STRICKLAND,**
**MARCY GEORGE,**
**JASON BISCHOFF,**
**ED LANE,**
**BETH ARTALE,**
AND **MICHAEL KELLY**

ABDO Spotlight
BOOM! STUDIOS
Licensed by: Hasbro

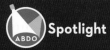

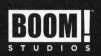

# ABDOBOOKS.COM

Reinforced library bound edition published in 2020 by Spotlight,
a division of ABDO, PO Box 398166, Minneapolis, Minnesota 55439.
Spotlight produces high-quality reinforced library bound editions for
schools and libraries. Published by agreement with BOOM! Studios.

Printed in the United States of America, North Mankato, Minnesota.
092019
012020

THIS BOOK CONTAINS
RECYCLED MATERIALS

Licensed by:

Library of Congress Control Number: 2019942386

Publisher's Cataloging-in-Publication Data

Names: Higgins, Kyle, author. | Prasetya, Hendry; Herms, Matt; Silas, Thony;
    Valenza, Bryan; illustrators.
Title: Mighty morphin power rangers/ writer: Kyle Higgins; art: Hendry Prasetya;
    Matt Herms; Thony Silas; Bryan Valenza.
Description: Minneapolis, Minnesota: Spotlight, 2020 | Series: Mighty morphin
    power rangers
Summary: Tommy Oliver was new in town when evil doer, Rita Repulsa, made him
    the Green Ranger. After escaping her mind control, he hopes for a normal life,
    which isn't easy to do with the plights of high school, making new friends, and
    the dangers that come with being a Power Ranger.
Identifiers: ISBN 9781532144233 (#1, lib. bdg.) | ISBN 9781532144240 (#2, lib.
    bdg.) | ISBN 9781532144257 (#3, lib. bdg.) | ISBN 9781532144264 (#4, lib.
    bdg.) | ISBN 9781532144271 (#5, lib. bdg.) | ISBN 9781532144288 (#6, lib.
    bdg.) | ISBN 9781532144295 (#7, lib. bdg.) | ISBN 9781532144301 (#8, lib.
    bdg.) | ISBN 9781532144318 (#9, lib. bdg.)
Subjects: LCSH: Mighty Morphin Power Rangers (Television program)--Juvenile
    fiction. | Ninjas--Juvenile fiction. | Superheroes--Juvenile fiction. | Good and
    evil--Juvenile fiction. | Graphic novels--Juvenile fiction. | Comic books, strips,
    etc.--Juvenile fiction
Classification: DDC 741.5--dc23

Spotlight

A Division of ABDO
abdobooks.com

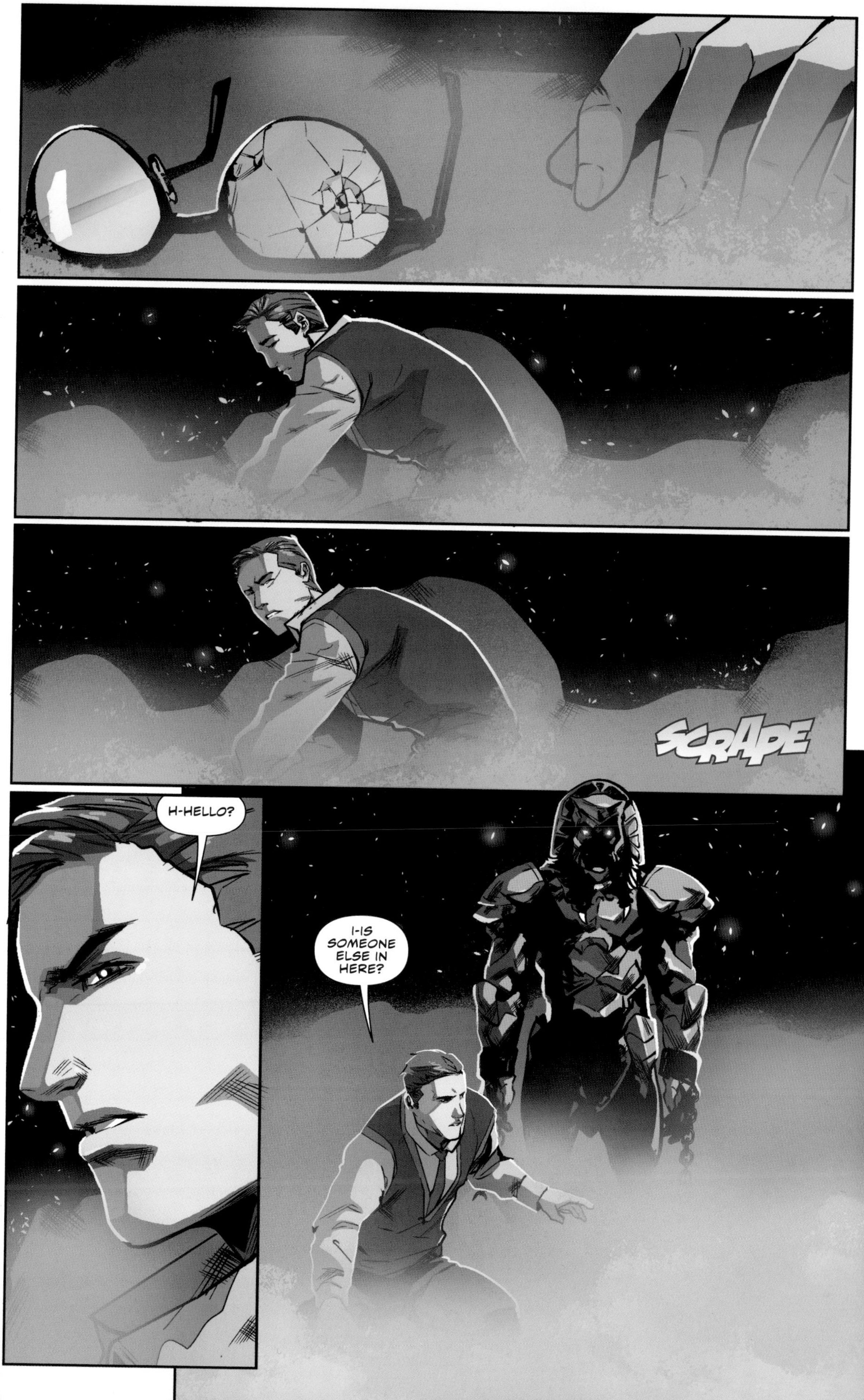
SCRAPE
H-HELLO?
I-IS SOMEONE ELSE IN HERE?

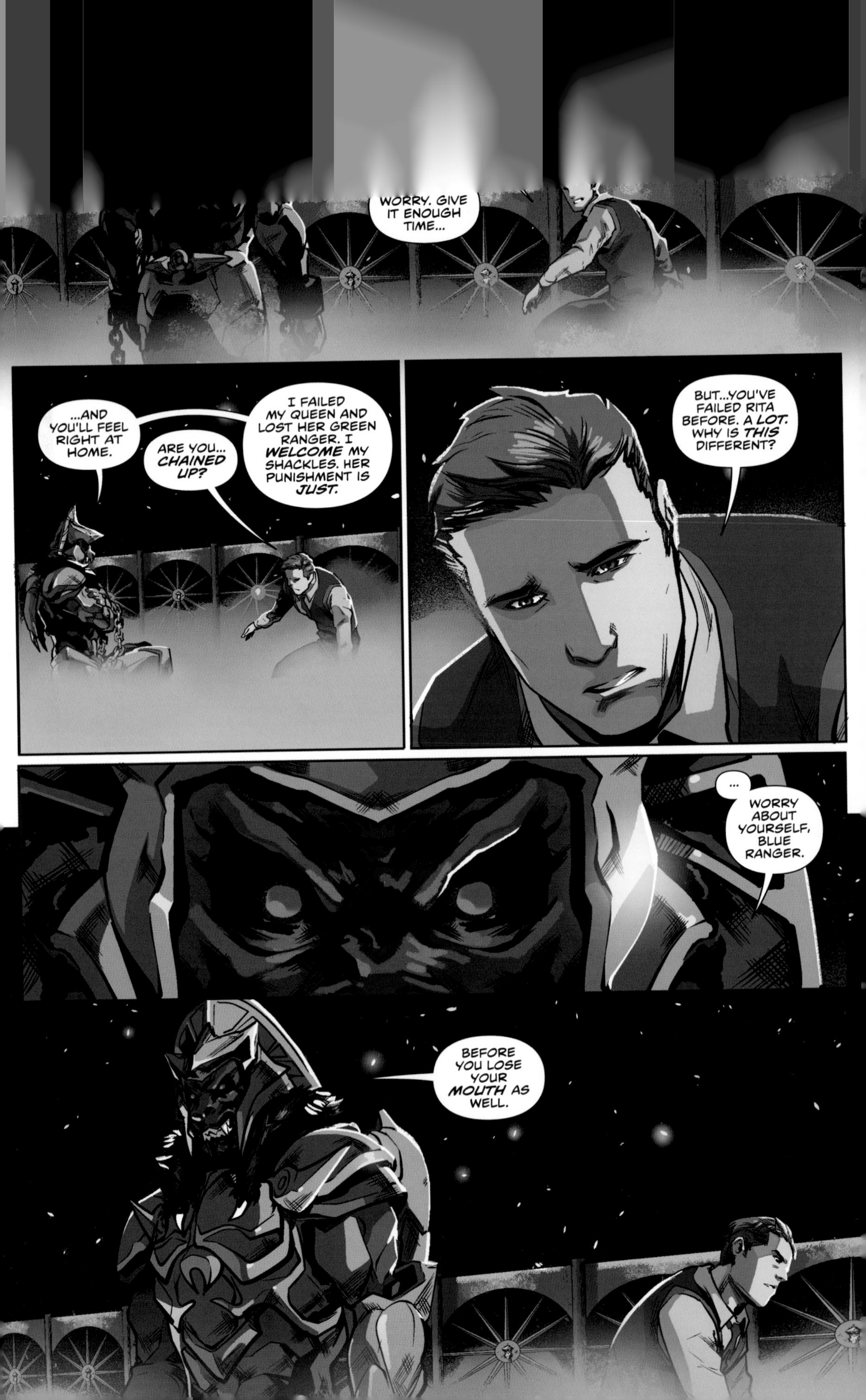
WORRY. GIVE IT ENOUGH TIME...
...AND YOU'LL FEEL RIGHT AT HOME.
ARE YOU... CHAINED UP?
I FAILED MY QUEEN AND LOST HER GREEN RANGER. I WELCOME MY SHACKLES. HER PUNISHMENT IS JUST.
BUT...YOU'VE FAILED RITA BEFORE. A LOT. WHY IS THIS DIFFERENT?
...
WORRY ABOUT YOURSELF, BLUE RANGER.
BEFORE YOU LOSE YOUR MOUTH AS WELL.

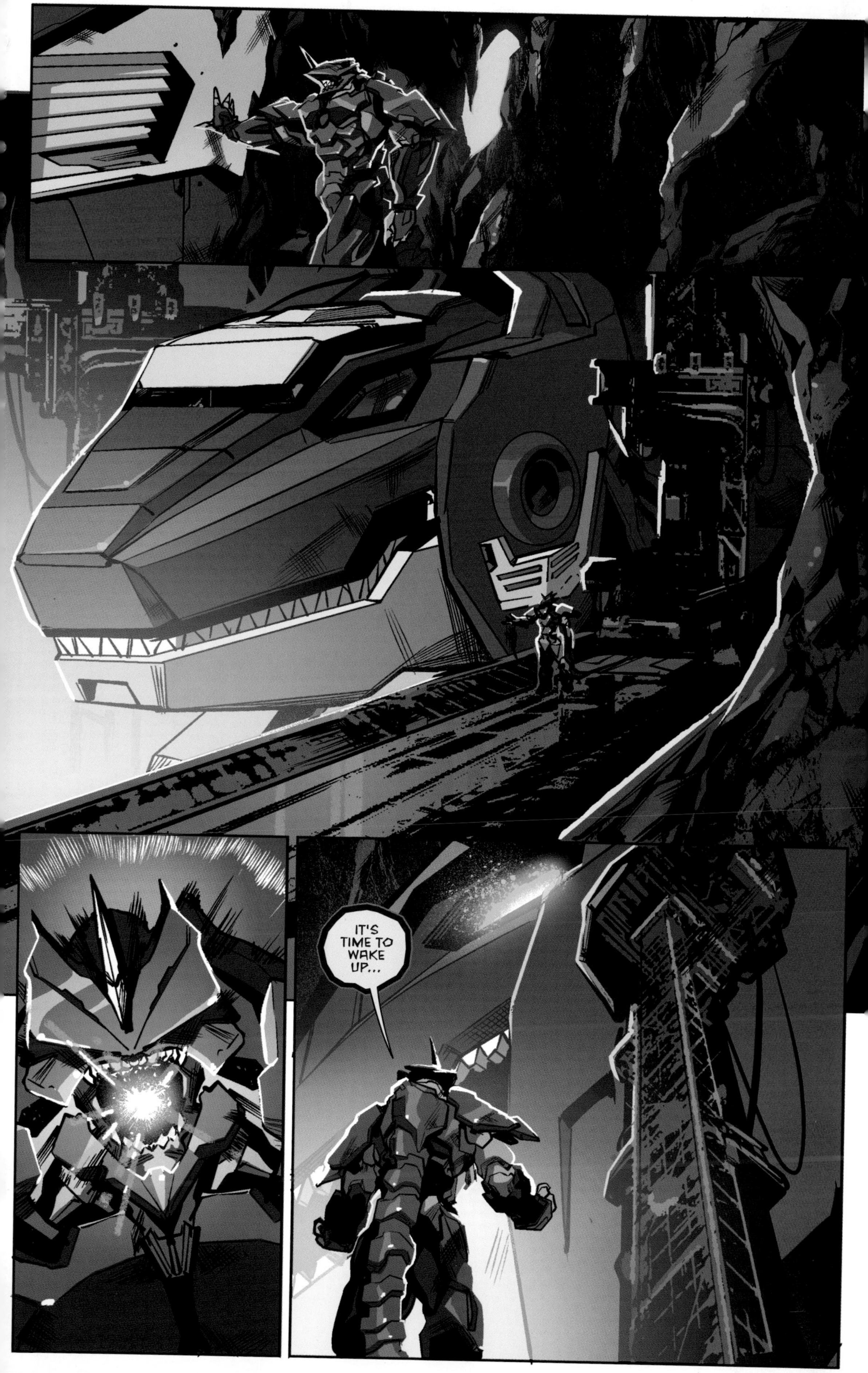
IT'S TIME TO WAKE UP...

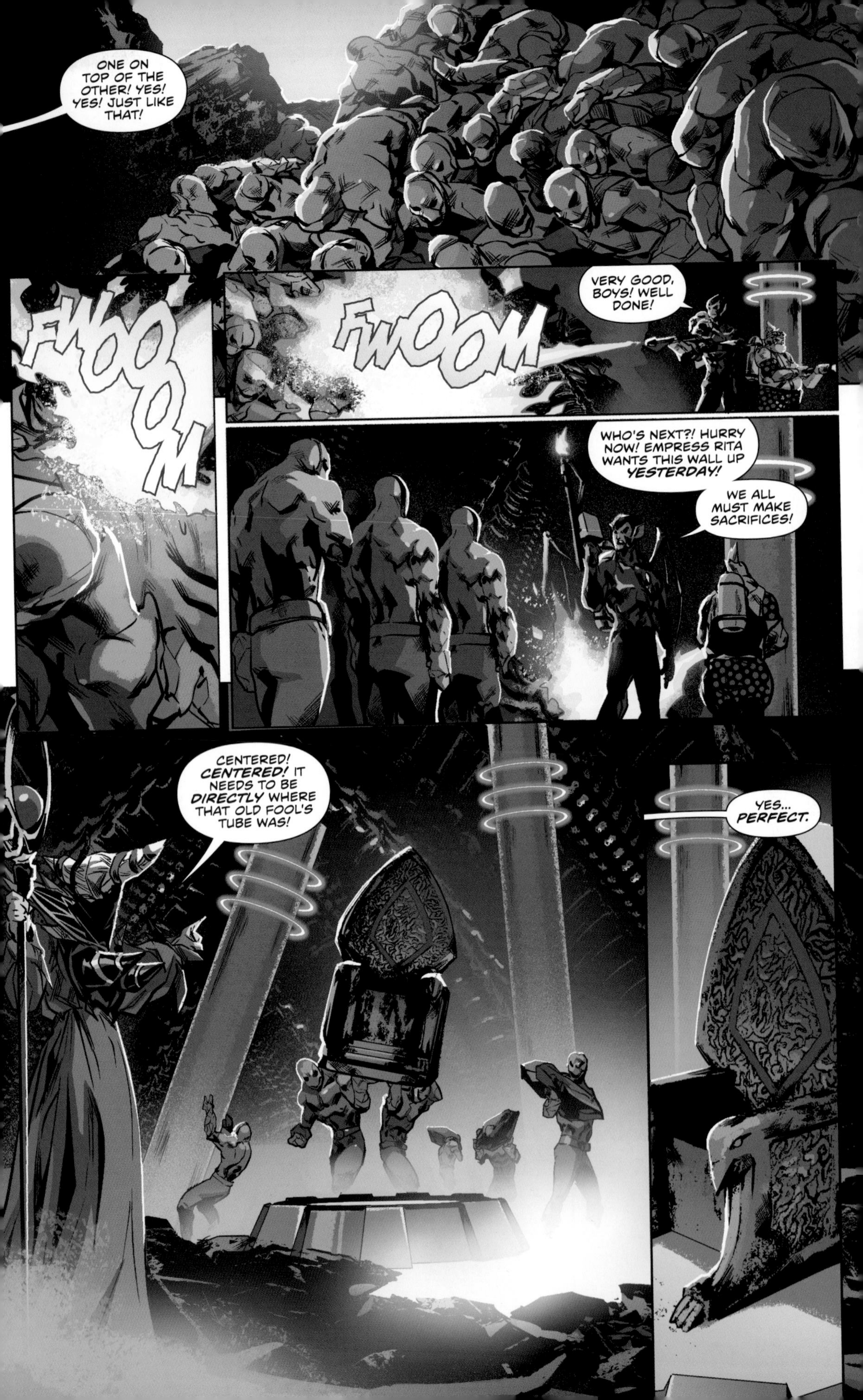
ONE ON TOP OF THE OTHER! YES! YES! JUST LIKE THAT!
FWOOOOM
FWOOM
VERY GOOD, BOYS! WELL DONE!
WHO'S NEXT?! HURRY NOW! EMPRESS RITA WANTS THIS WALL UP YESTERDAY!
WE ALL MUST MAKE SACRIFICES!
CENTERED! CENTERED! IT NEEDS TO BE DIRECTLY WHERE THAT OLD FOOL'S TUBE WAS!
YES... PERFECT.

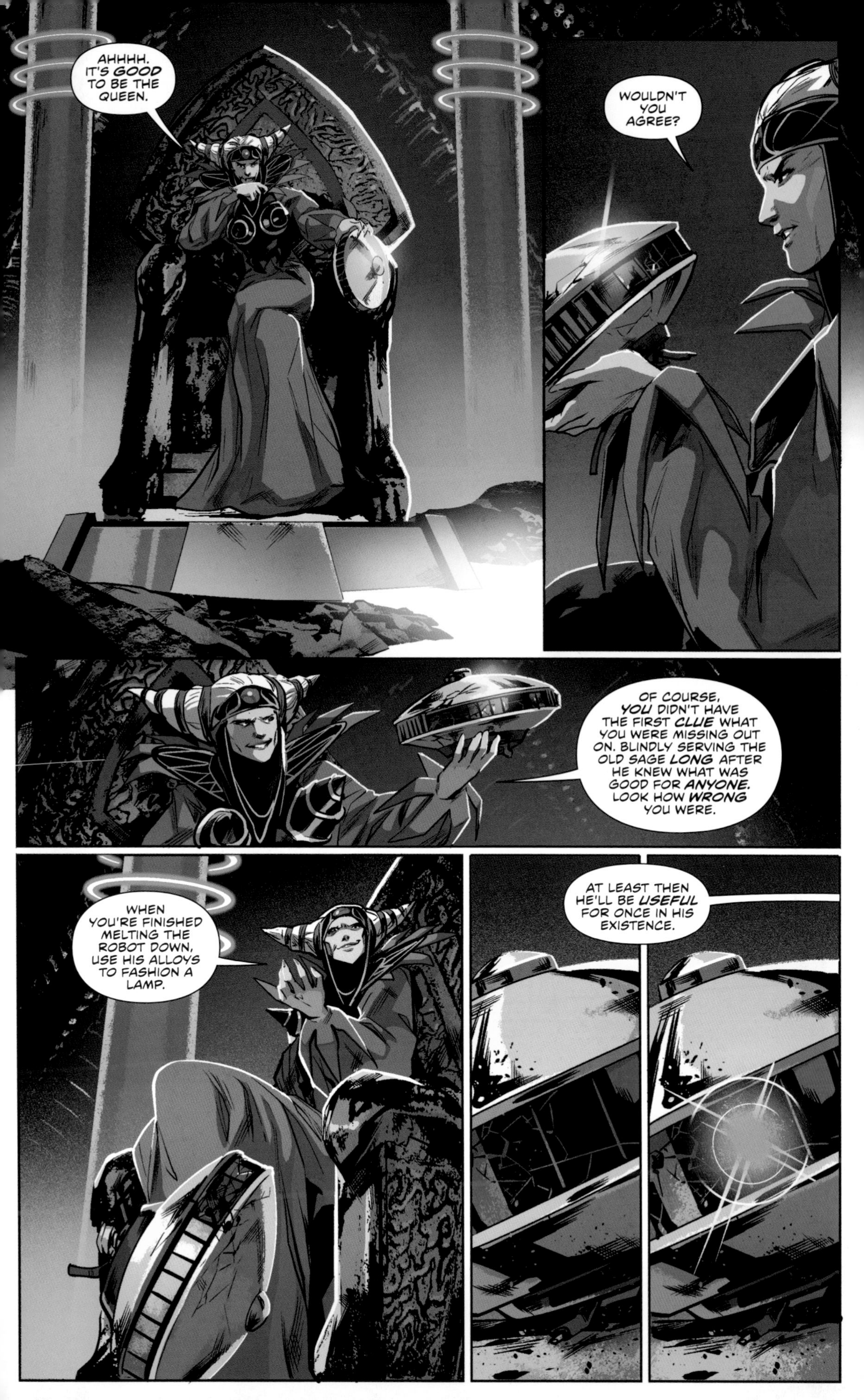
AHHHH. IT'S GOOD TO BE THE QUEEN.
WOULDN'T YOU AGREE?
OF COURSE, YOU DIDN'T HAVE THE FIRST CLUE WHAT YOU WERE MISSING OUT ON. BLINDLY SERVING THE OLD SAGE LONG AFTER HE KNEW WHAT WAS GOOD FOR ANYONE. LOOK HOW WRONG YOU WERE.
WHEN YOU'RE FINISHED MELTING THE ROBOT DOWN, USE HIS ALLOYS TO FASHION A LAMP.
AT LEAST THEN HE'LL BE USEFUL FOR ONCE IN HIS EXISTENCE.

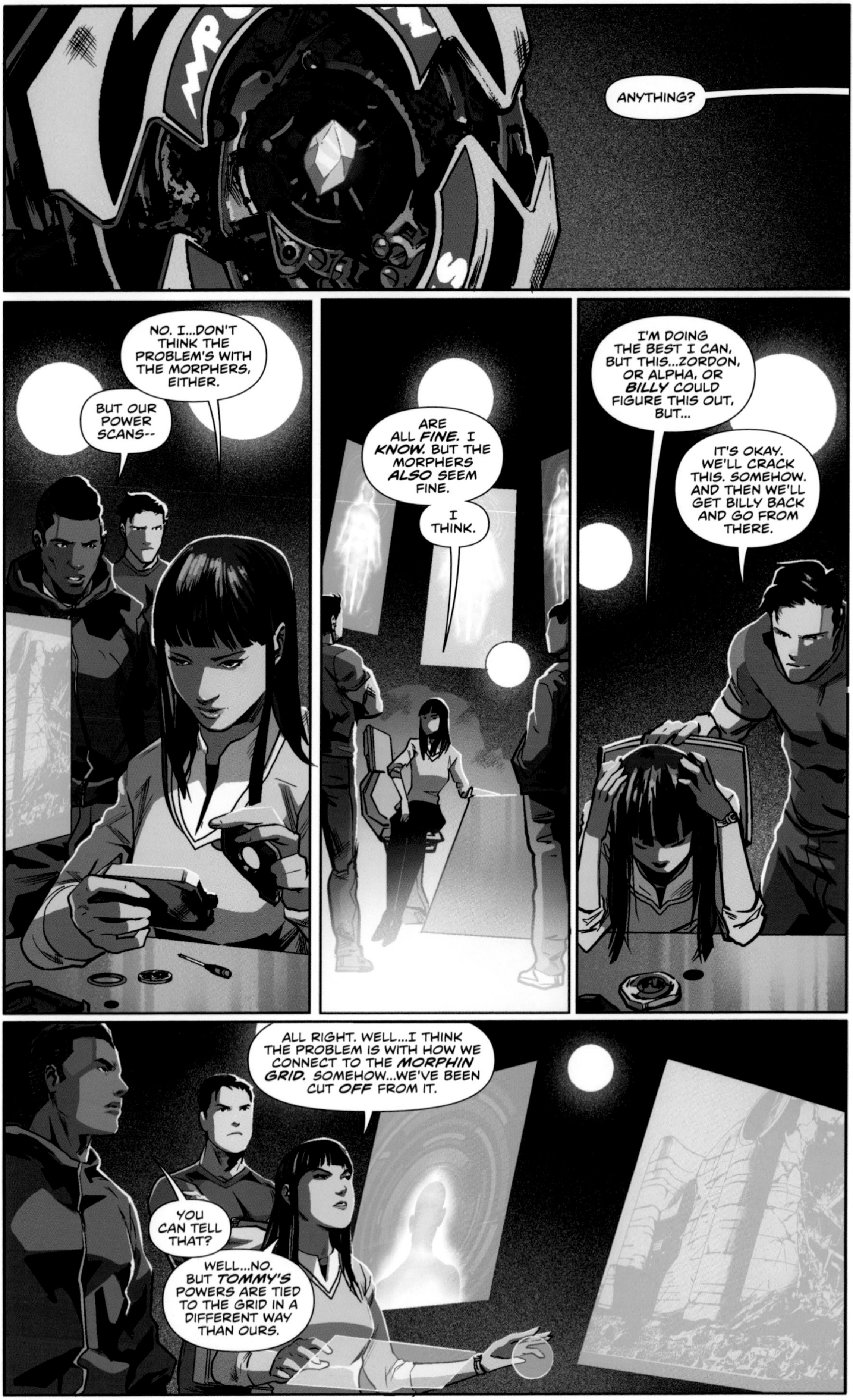
ANYTHING?
NO. I...DON'T THINK THE PROBLEM'S WITH THE MORPHERS, EITHER.
BUT OUR POWER SCANS--
ARE ALL FINE. I KNOW. BUT THE MORPHERS ALSO SEEM FINE.
I THINK.
I'M DOING THE BEST I CAN, BUT THIS...ZORDON, OR ALPHA, OR BILLY COULD FIGURE THIS OUT, BUT...
IT'S OKAY. WE'LL CRACK THIS. SOMEHOW. AND THEN WE'LL GET BILLY BACK AND GO FROM THERE.
ALL RIGHT. WELL...I THINK THE PROBLEM IS WITH HOW WE CONNECT TO THE MORPHIN GRID. SOMEHOW...WE'VE BEEN CUT OFF FROM IT.
YOU CAN TELL THAT?
WELL...NO. BUT TOMMY'S POWERS ARE TIED TO THE GRID IN A DIFFERENT WAY THAN OURS.

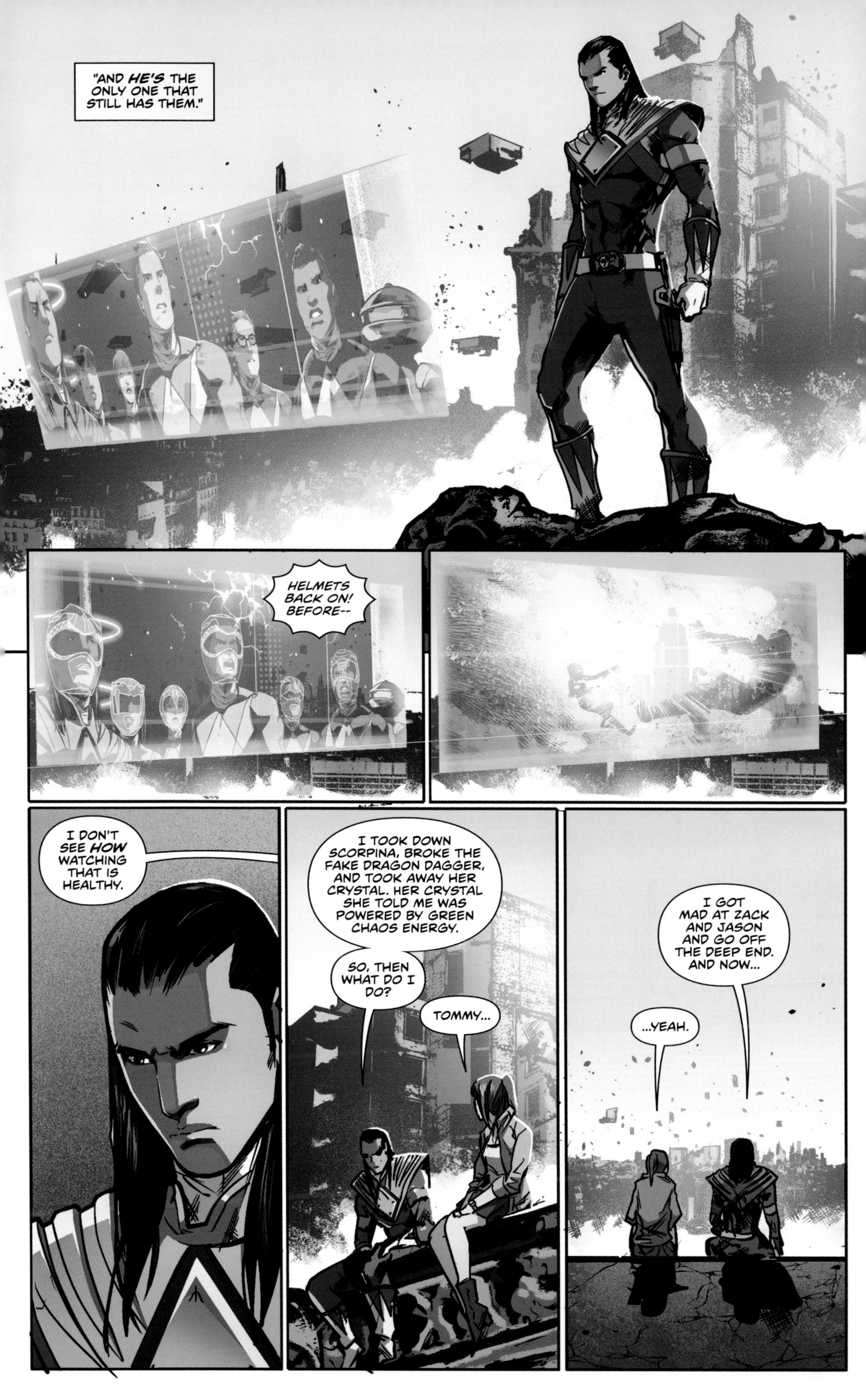
"AND HE'S THE ONLY ONE THAT STILL HAS THEM."
HELMETS BACK ON! BEFORE--
I DON'T SEE HOW WATCHING THAT IS HEALTHY.
I TOOK DOWN SCORPINA, BROKE THE FAKE DRAGON DAGGER, AND TOOK AWAY HER CRYSTAL. HER CRYSTAL SHE TOLD ME WAS POWERED BY GREEN CHAOS ENERGY.
SO, THEN WHAT DO I DO?
TOMMY...
I GOT MAD AT ZACK AND JASON AND GO OFF THE DEEP END. AND NOW...
...YEAH.

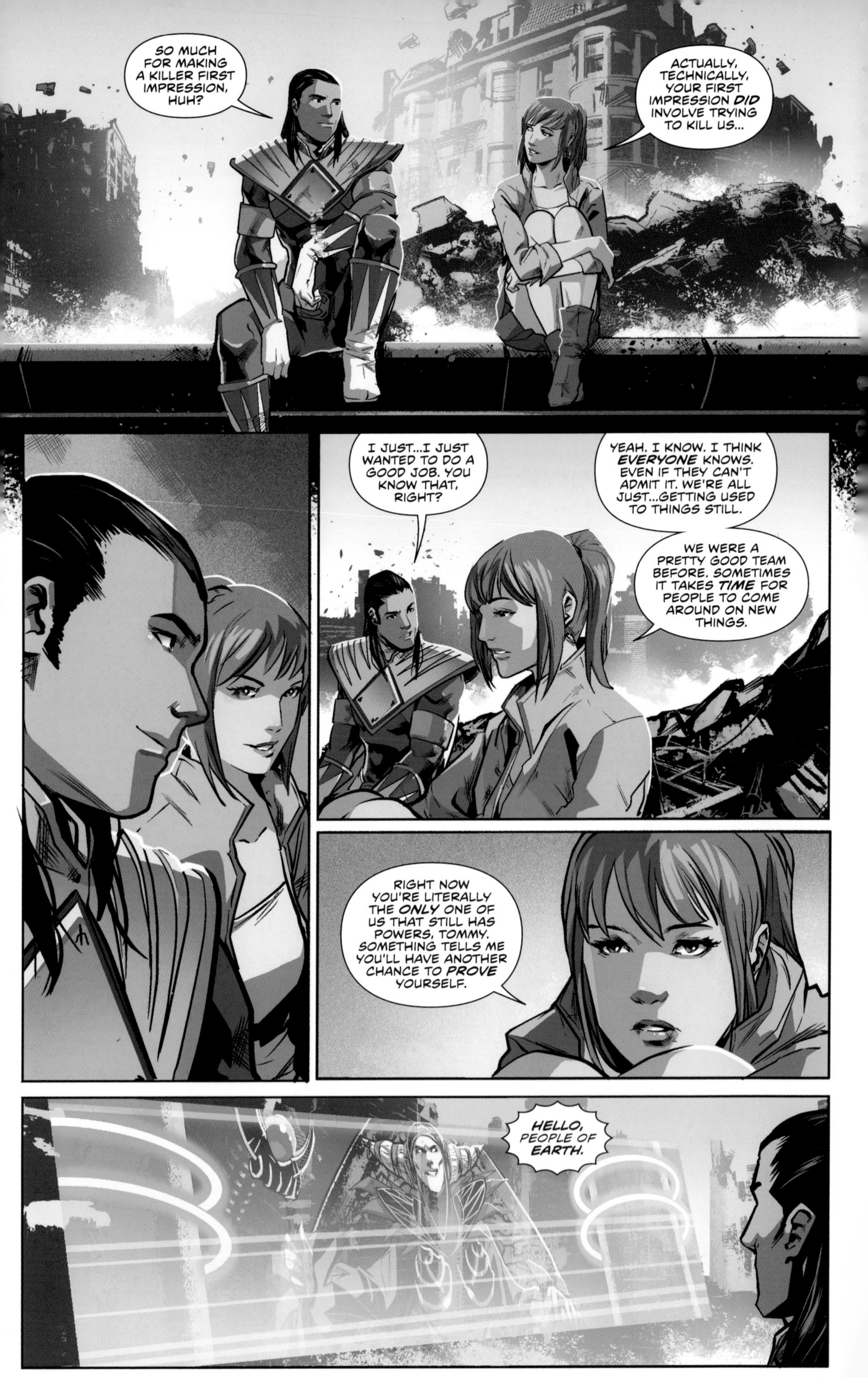
SO MUCH FOR MAKING A KILLER FIRST IMPRESSION, HUH?
ACTUALLY, TECHNICALLY, YOUR FIRST IMPRESSION DID INVOLVE TRYING TO KILL US...
I JUST...I JUST WANTED TO DO A GOOD JOB. YOU KNOW THAT, RIGHT?
YEAH. I KNOW. I THINK EVERYONE KNOWS. EVEN IF THEY CAN'T ADMIT IT. WE'RE ALL JUST...GETTING USED TO THINGS STILL.
WE WERE A PRETTY GOOD TEAM BEFORE. SOMETIMES IT TAKES TIME FOR PEOPLE TO COME AROUND ON NEW THINGS.
RIGHT NOW YOU'RE LITERALLY THE ONLY ONE OF US THAT STILL HAS POWERS, TOMMY. SOMETHING TELLS ME YOU'LL HAVE ANOTHER CHANCE TO PROVE YOURSELF.
HELLO, PEOPLE OF EARTH.

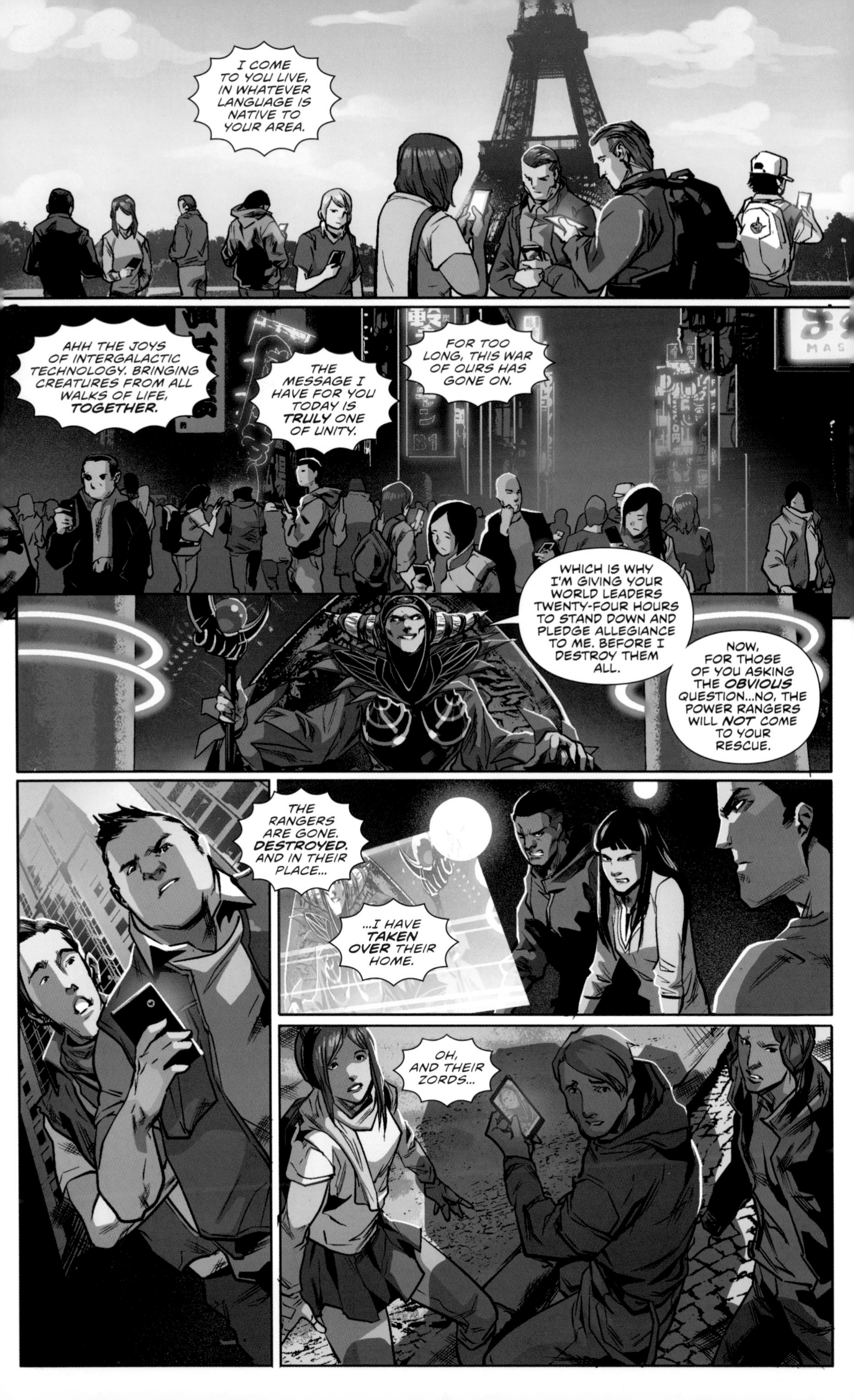
I COME TO YOU LIVE, IN WHATEVER LANGUAGE IS NATIVE TO YOUR AREA.
AHH THE JOYS OF INTERGALACTIC TECHNOLOGY. BRINGING CREATURES FROM ALL WALKS OF LIFE, TOGETHER.
THE MESSAGE I HAVE FOR YOU TODAY IS TRULY ONE OF UNITY.
FOR TOO LONG, THIS WAR OF OURS HAS GONE ON.
WHICH IS WHY I'M GIVING YOUR WORLD LEADERS TWENTY-FOUR HOURS TO STAND DOWN AND PLEDGE ALLEGIANCE TO ME. BEFORE I DESTROY THEM ALL.
NOW, FOR THOSE OF YOU ASKING THE OBVIOUS QUESTION...NO, THE POWER RANGERS WILL NOT COME TO YOUR RESCUE.
THE RANGERS ARE GONE. DESTROYED. AND IN THEIR PLACE...
...I HAVE TAKEN OVER THEIR HOME.
OH, AND THEIR ZORDS...

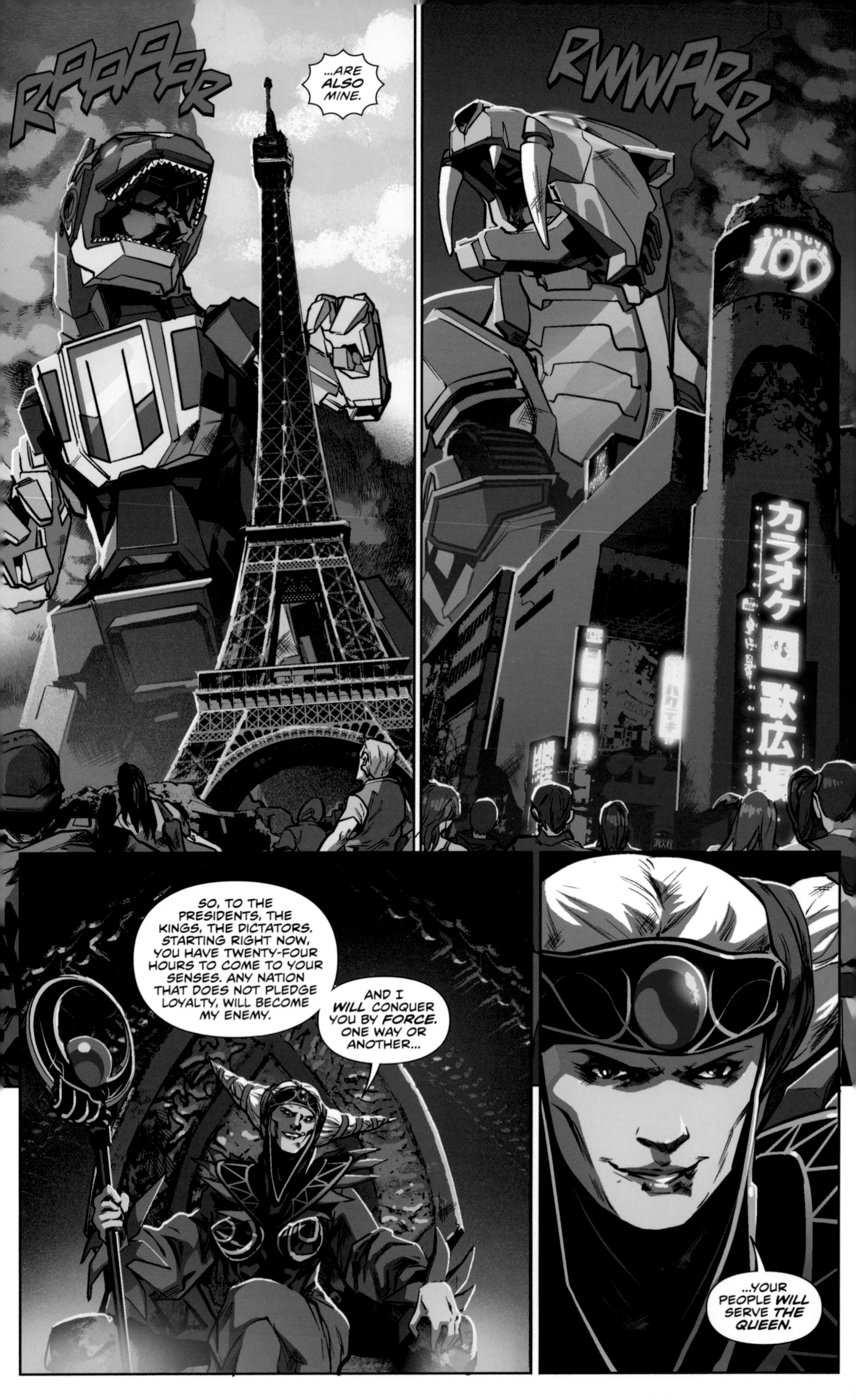
RAAAAR
...ARE ALSO MINE.
RWWARR
SHIBUYA 109
カラオケ
歌広場
SO, TO THE PRESIDENTS, THE KINGS, THE DICTATORS. STARTING RIGHT NOW, YOU HAVE TWENTY-FOUR HOURS TO COME TO YOUR SENSES. ANY NATION THAT DOES NOT PLEDGE LOYALTY, WILL BECOME MY ENEMY.
AND I WILL CONQUER YOU BY FORCE. ONE WAY OR ANOTHER...
...YOUR PEOPLE WILL SERVE THE QUEEN.

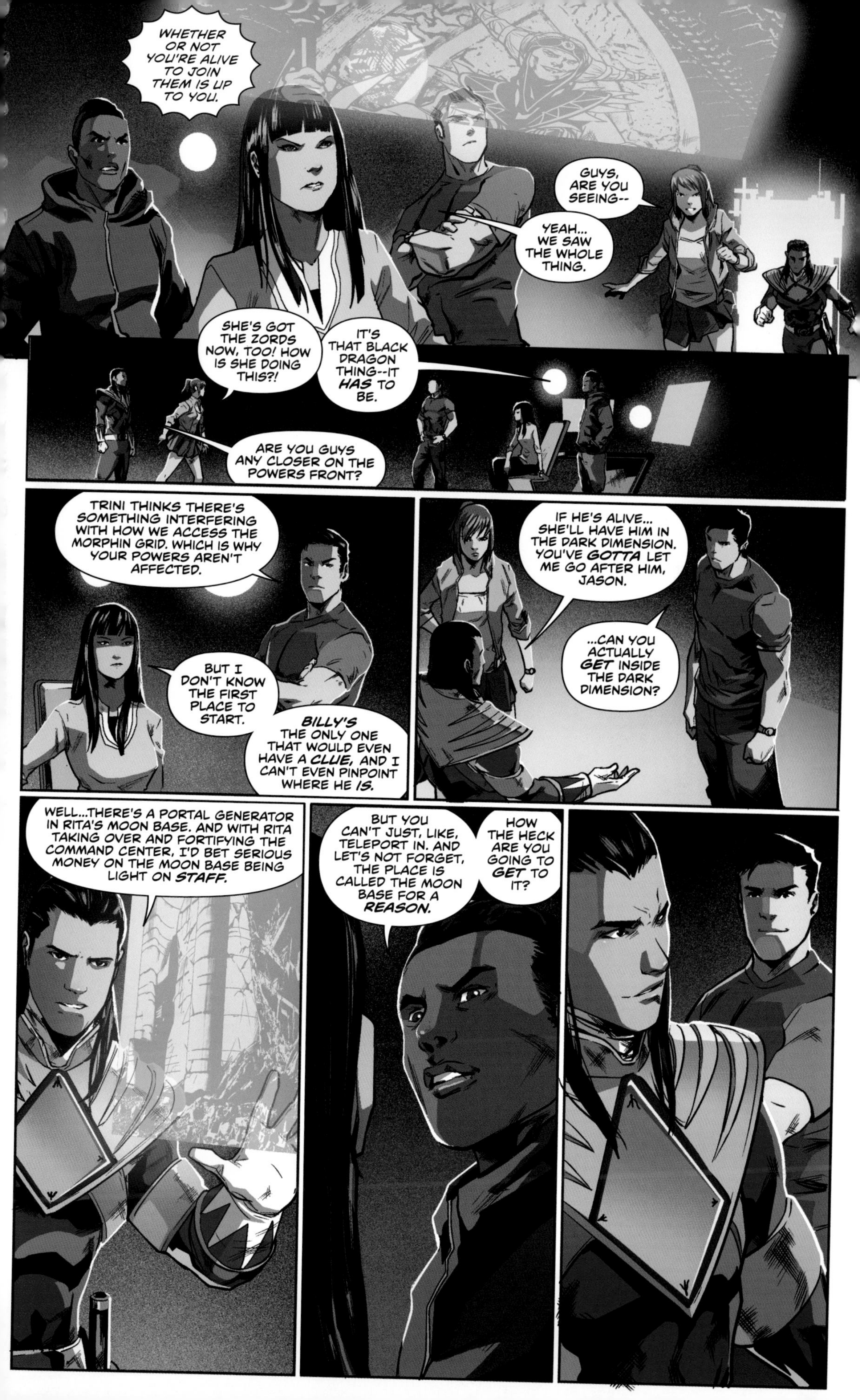
WHETHER OR NOT YOU'RE ALIVE TO JOIN THEM IS UP TO YOU.
GUYS, ARE YOU SEEING--
YEAH... WE SAW THE WHOLE THING.
SHE'S GOT THE ZORDS NOW, TOO! HOW IS SHE DOING THIS?!
IT'S THAT BLACK DRAGON THING--IT HAS TO BE.
ARE YOU GUYS ANY CLOSER ON THE POWERS FRONT?
TRINI THINKS THERE'S SOMETHING INTERFERING WITH HOW WE ACCESS THE MORPHIN GRID. WHICH IS WHY YOUR POWERS AREN'T AFFECTED.
BUT I DON'T KNOW THE FIRST PLACE TO START.
BILLY'S THE ONLY ONE THAT WOULD EVEN HAVE A CLUE, AND I CAN'T EVEN PINPOINT WHERE HE IS.
IF HE'S ALIVE... SHE'LL HAVE HIM IN THE DARK DIMENSION. YOU'VE GOTTA LET ME GO AFTER HIM, JASON.
...CAN YOU ACTUALLY GET INSIDE THE DARK DIMENSION?
WELL...THERE'S A PORTAL GENERATOR IN RITA'S MOON BASE. AND WITH RITA TAKING OVER AND FORTIFYING THE COMMAND CENTER, I'D BET SERIOUS MONEY ON THE MOON BASE BEING LIGHT ON STAFF.
BUT YOU CAN'T JUST, LIKE, TELEPORT IN. AND LET'S NOT FORGET, THE PLACE IS CALLED THE MOON BASE FOR A REASON.
HOW THE HECK ARE YOU GOING TO GET TO IT?

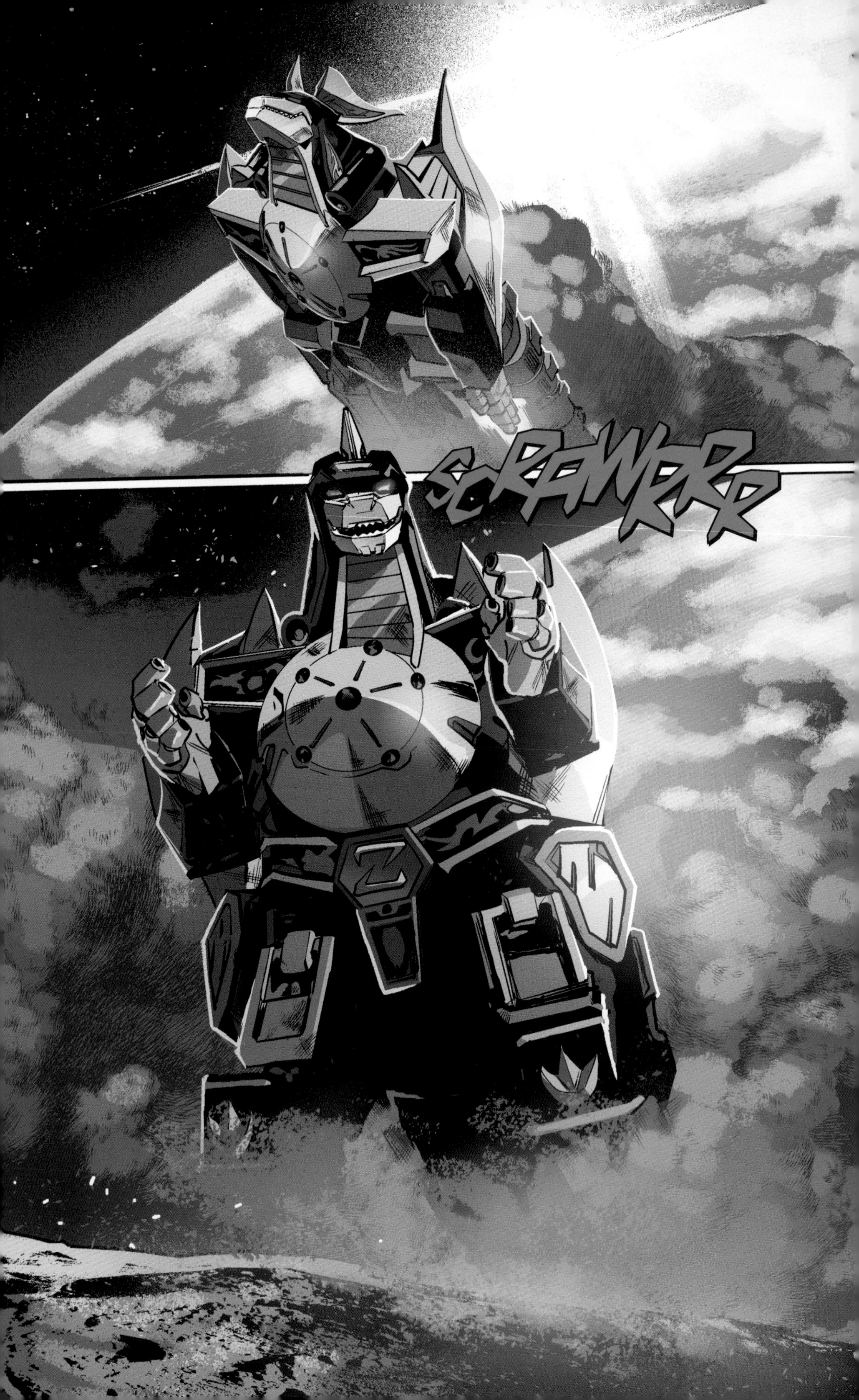
SCRAWRRR

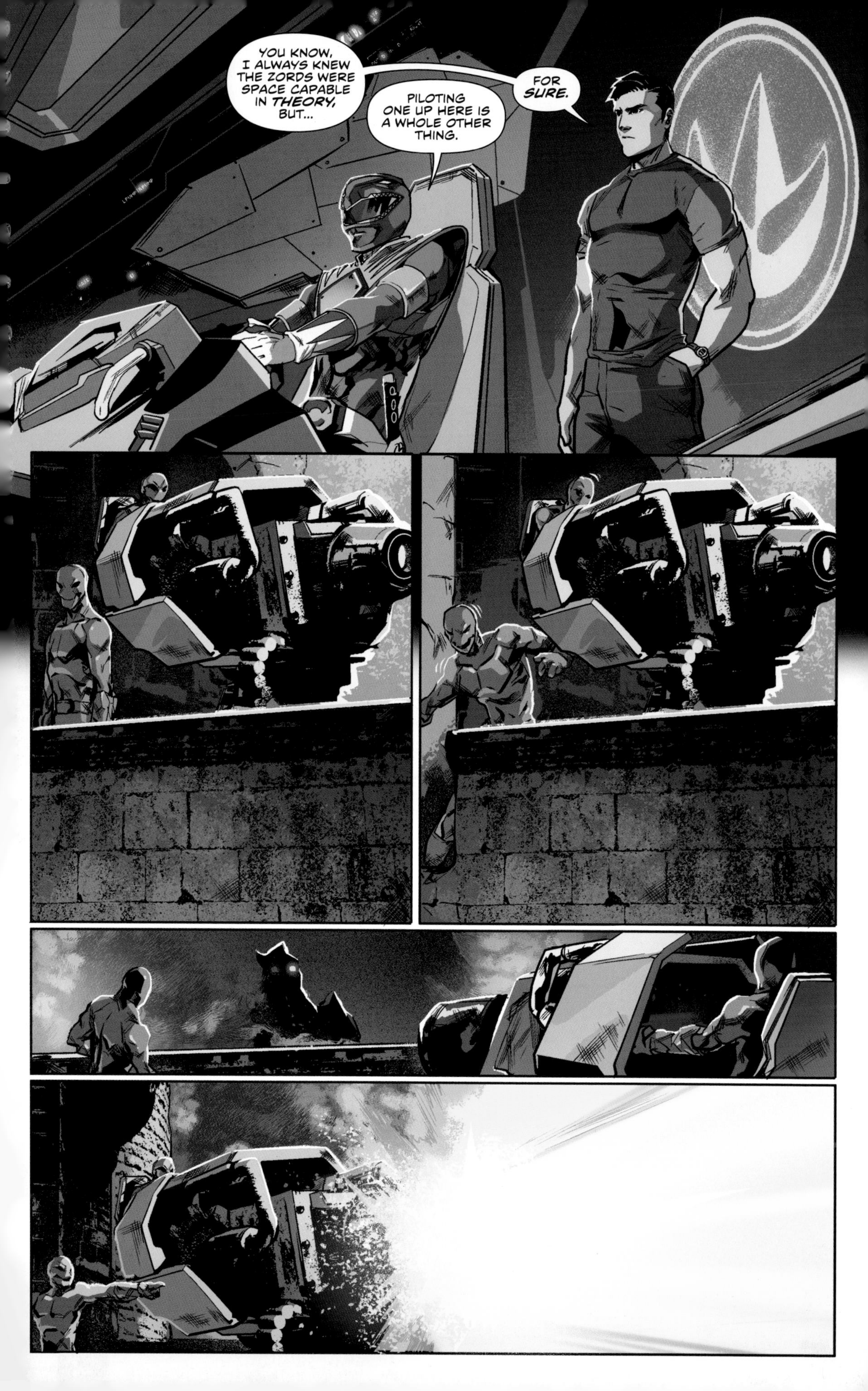
YOU KNOW, I ALWAYS KNEW THE ZORDS WERE SPACE CAPABLE IN *THEORY*, BUT...
FOR *SURE*.
PILOTING ONE UP HERE IS A WHOLE OTHER THING.

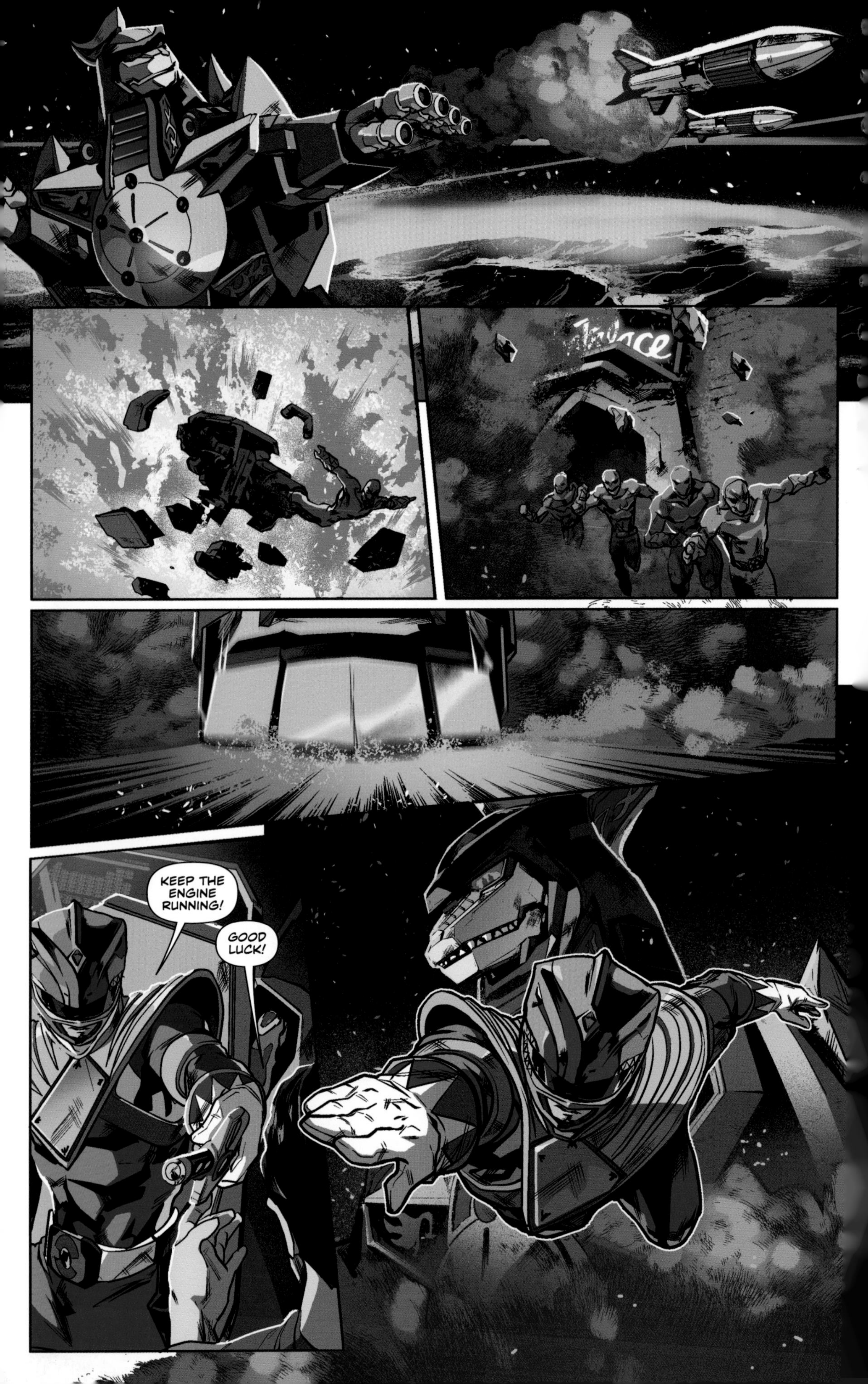
KEEP THE ENGINE RUNNING!
GOOD LUCK!

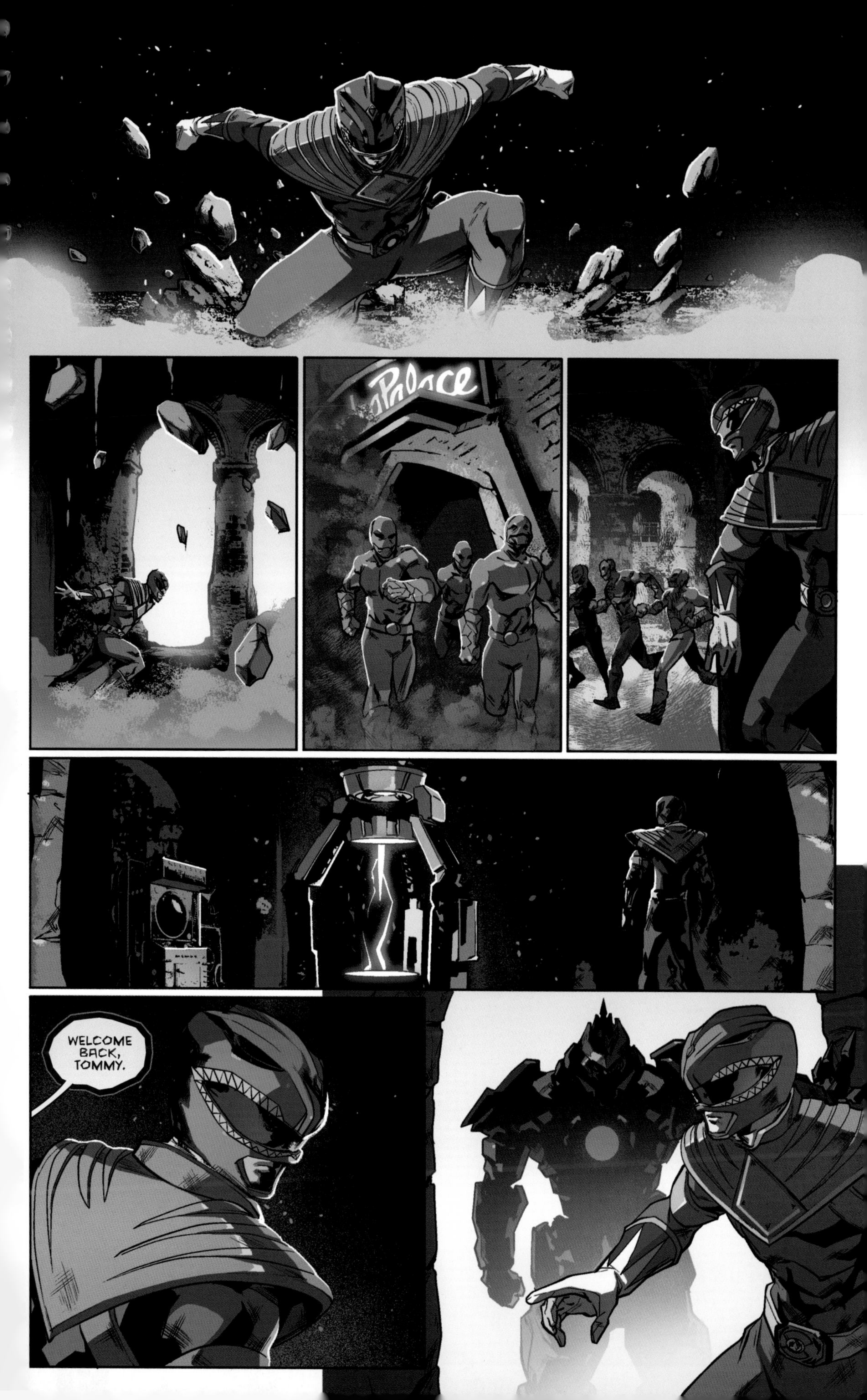
Palace
WELCOME BACK, TOMMY.

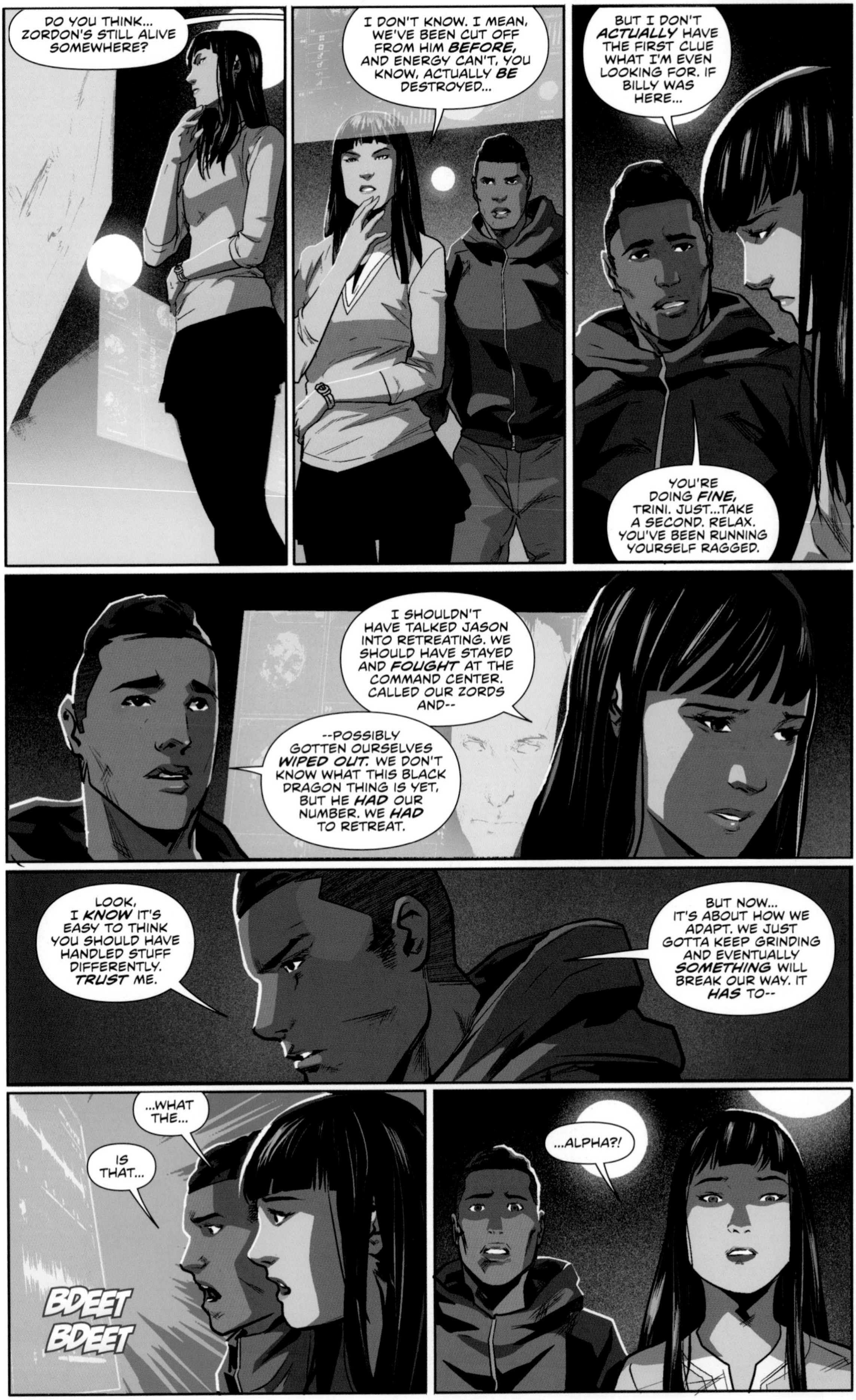
DO YOU THINK... ZORDON'S STILL ALIVE SOMEWHERE?
I DON'T KNOW. I MEAN, WE'VE BEEN CUT OFF FROM HIM BEFORE, AND ENERGY CAN'T, YOU KNOW, ACTUALLY BE DESTROYED...
BUT I DON'T ACTUALLY HAVE THE FIRST CLUE WHAT I'M EVEN LOOKING FOR. IF BILLY WAS HERE...
YOU'RE DOING FINE, TRINI. JUST...TAKE A SECOND. RELAX. YOU'VE BEEN RUNNING YOURSELF RAGGED.
I SHOULDN'T HAVE TALKED JASON INTO RETREATING. WE SHOULD HAVE STAYED AND FOUGHT AT THE COMMAND CENTER. CALLED OUR ZORDS AND--
--POSSIBLY GOTTEN OURSELVES WIPED OUT. WE DON'T KNOW WHAT THIS BLACK DRAGON THING IS YET, BUT HE HAD OUR NUMBER. WE HAD TO RETREAT.
LOOK, I KNOW IT'S EASY TO THINK YOU SHOULD HAVE HANDLED STUFF DIFFERENTLY. TRUST ME.
BUT NOW... IT'S ABOUT HOW WE ADAPT. WE JUST GOTTA KEEP GRINDING AND EVENTUALLY SOMETHING WILL BREAK OUR WAY. IT HAS TO--
...WHAT THE...
IS THAT...
BDEET BDEET
...ALPHA?!

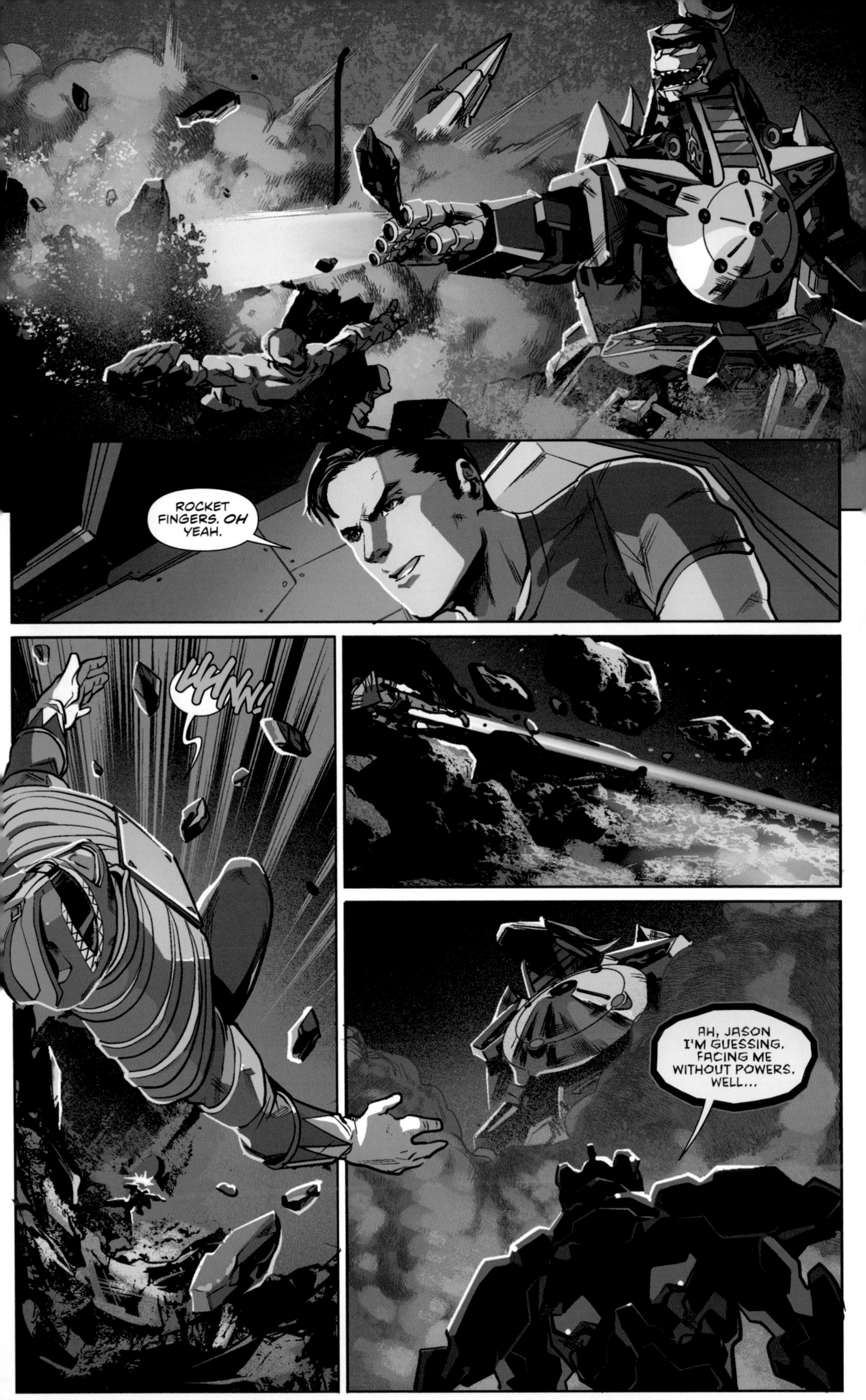
ROCKET FINGERS. OH YEAH.
WHNN!
AH, JASON I'M GUESSING. FACING ME WITHOUT POWERS. WELL...

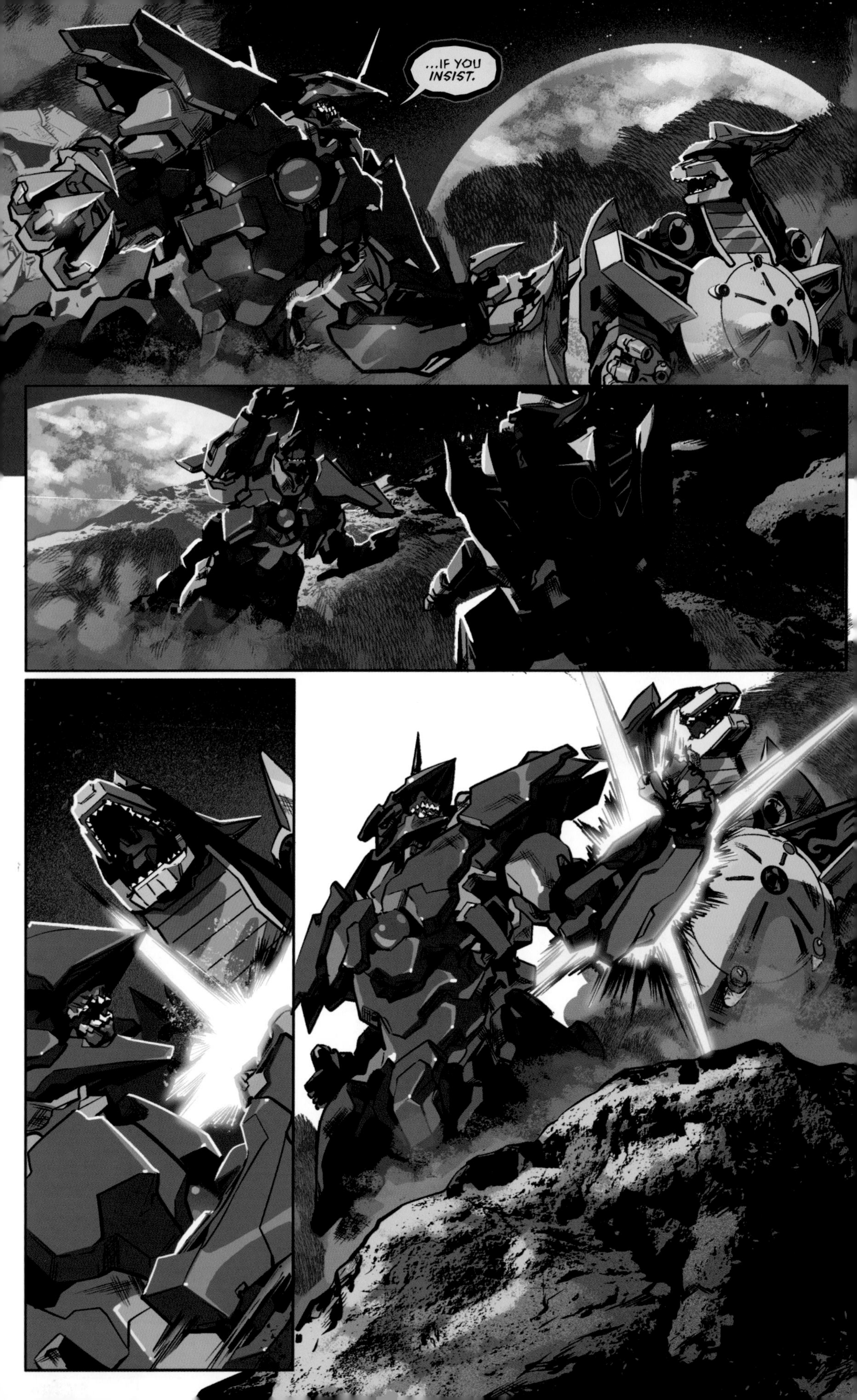
...IF YOU INSIST.

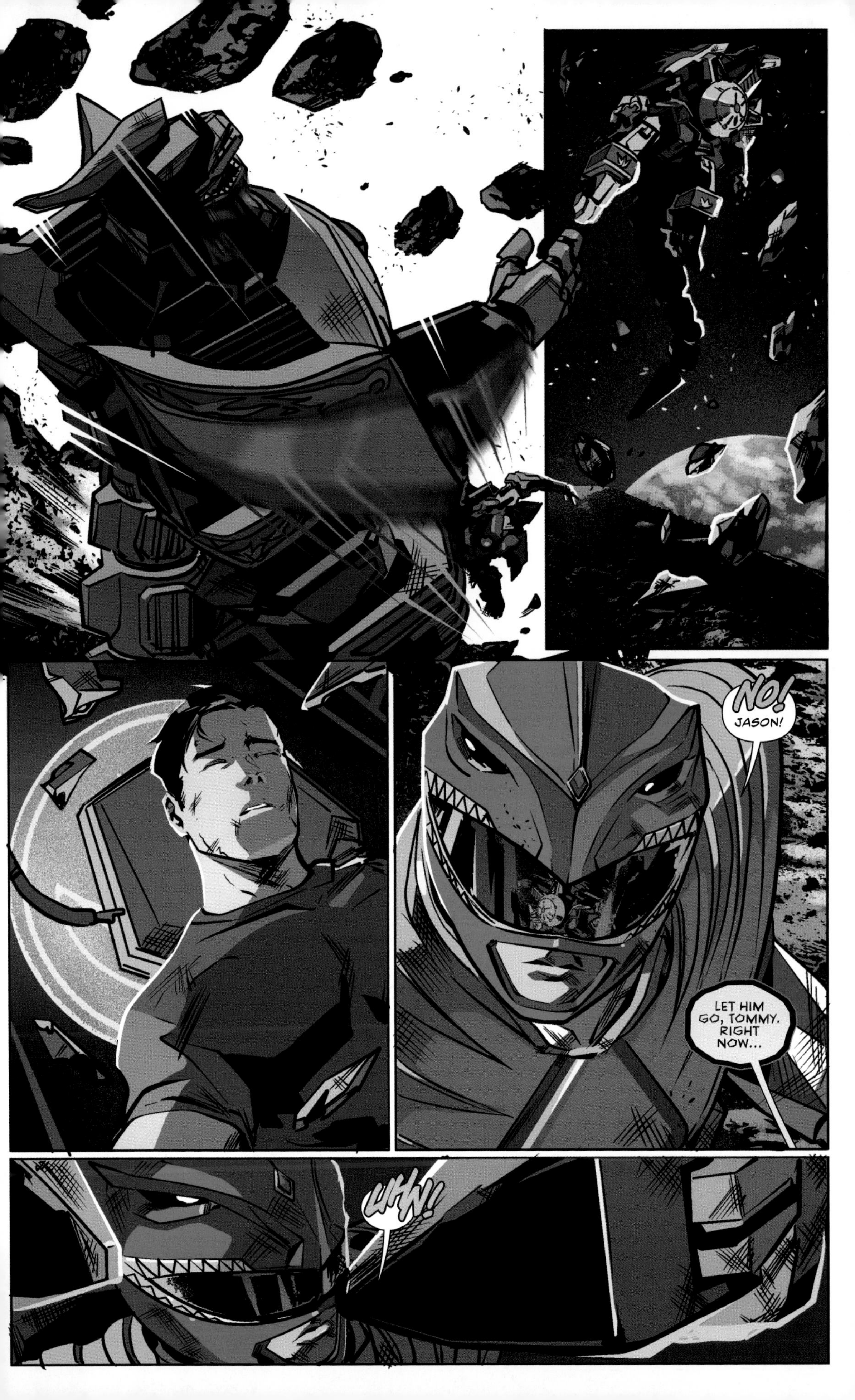
NO! JASON!
LET HIM GO, TOMMY. RIGHT NOW...
UHN!

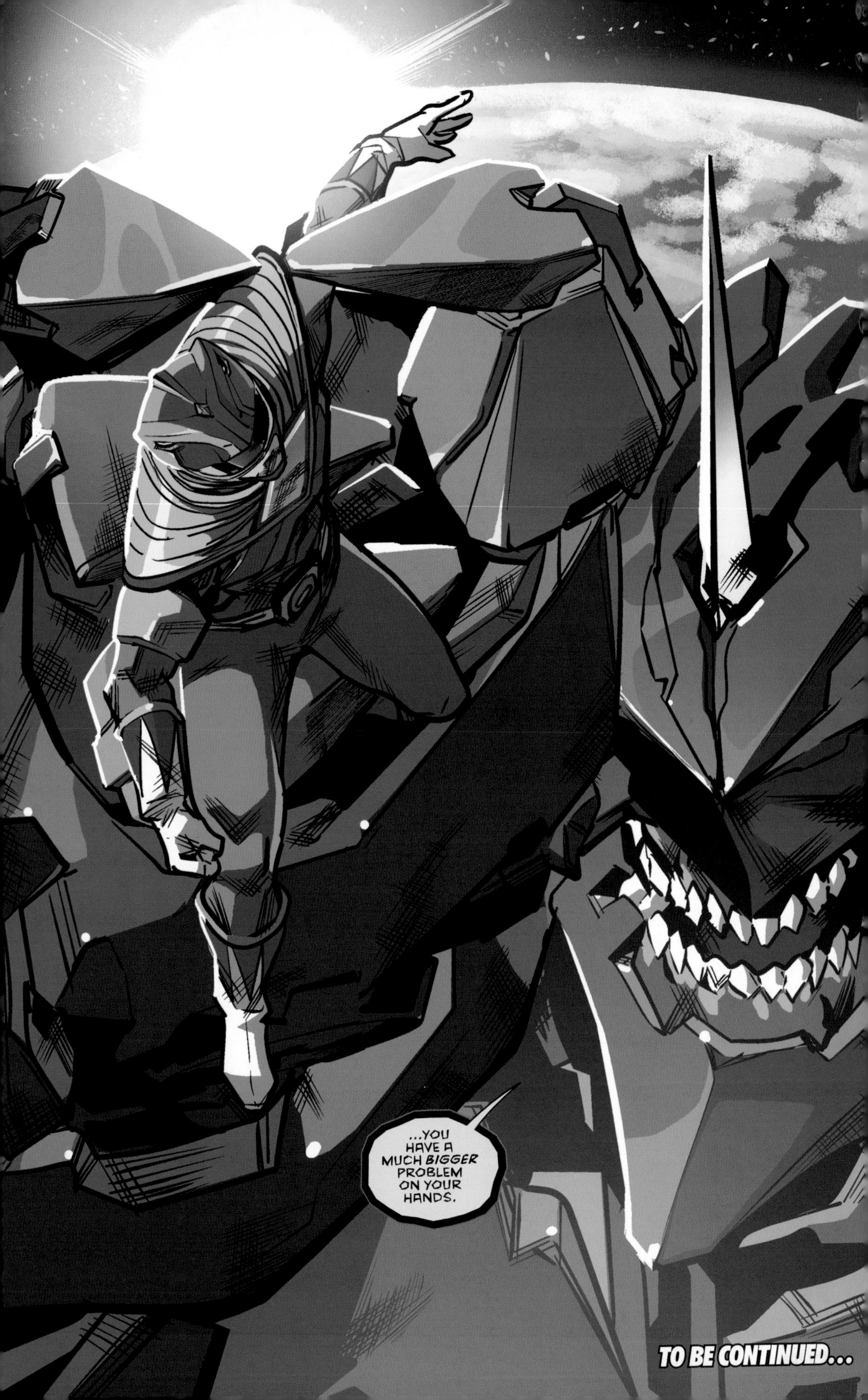
...YOU HAVE A MUCH BIGGER PROBLEM ON YOUR HANDS.
TO BE CONTINUED...

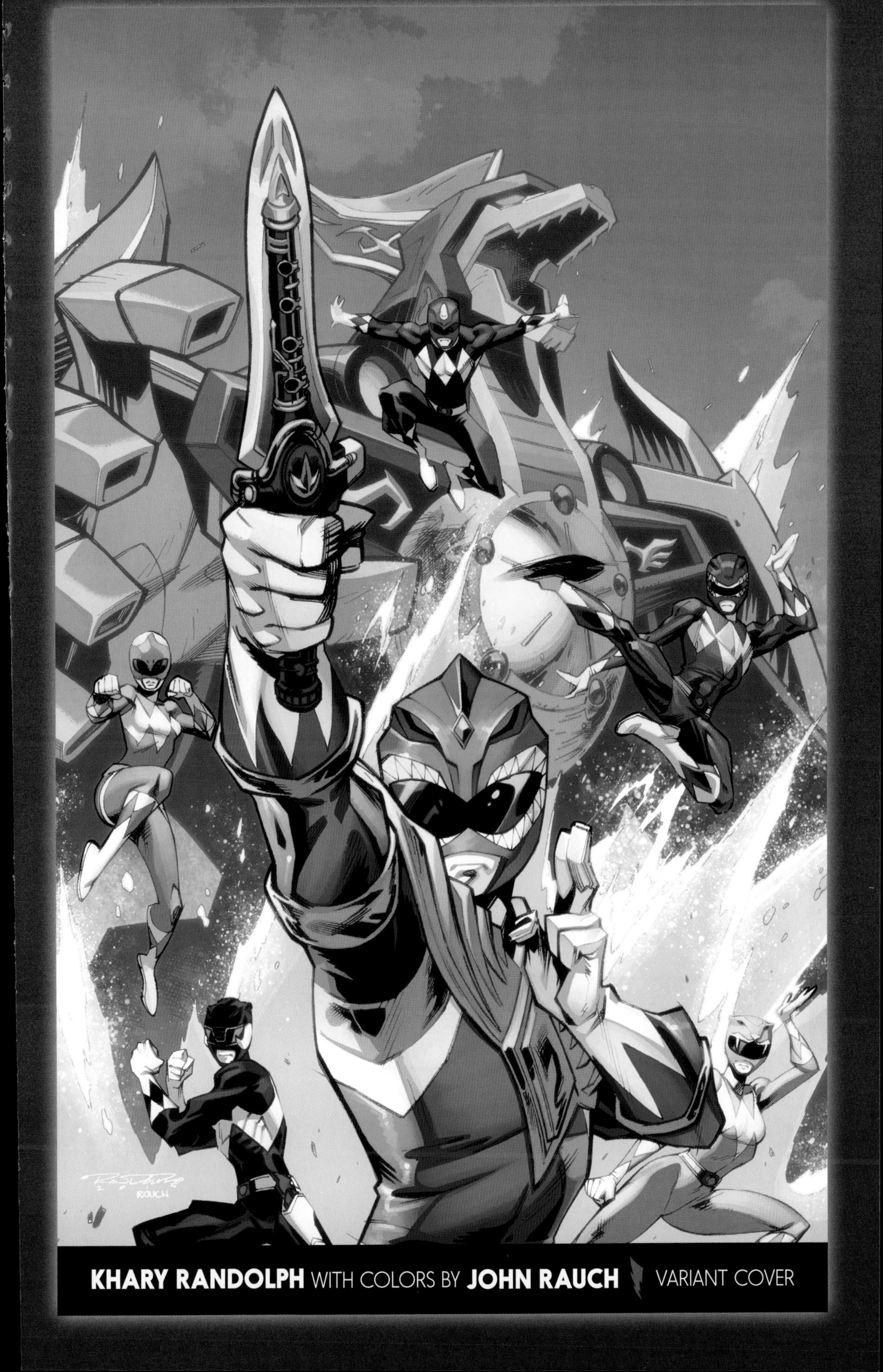

**KHARY RANDOLPH** WITH COLORS BY **JOHN RAUCH** VARIANT COVER

SABAN'S

# MIGHTY MORPHIN POWER RANGERS

## COLLECT THEM ALL!

**Set of 9 Hardcover Books ISBN: 978-1-5321-4422-6**

1
MIGHTY MORPHIN POWER RANGERS

Hardcover Book ISBN
978-1-5321-4423-3

2
MIGHTY MORPHIN POWER RANGERS

Hardcover Book ISBN
978-1-5321-4424-0

3
MIGHTY MORPHIN POWER RANGERS

Hardcover Book ISBN
978-1-5321-4425-7

4
MIGHTY MORPHIN POWER RANGERS

Hardcover Book ISBN
978-1-5321-4426-4

5
MIGHTY MORPHIN POWER RANGERS

Hardcover Book ISBN
978-1-5321-4427-1

6
MIGHTY MORPHIN POWER RANGERS

Hardcover Book ISBN
978-1-5321-4428-8

7
MIGHTY MORPHIN POWER RANGERS

Hardcover Book ISBN
978-1-5321-4429-5

8
MIGHTY MORPHIN POWER RANGERS

Hardcover Book ISBN
978-1-5321-4430-1

9
MIGHTY MORPHIN POWER RANGERS

Hardcover Book ISBN
978-1-5321-4431-8

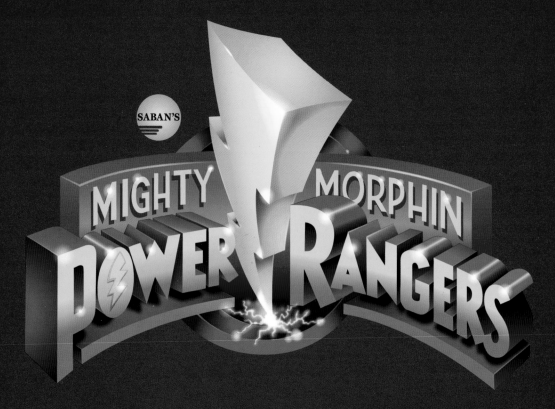

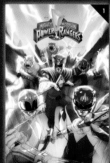

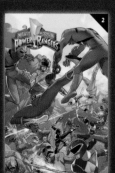

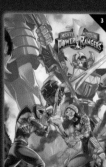

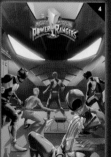

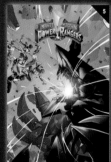

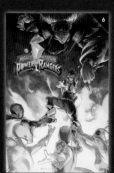

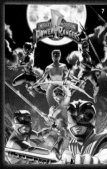

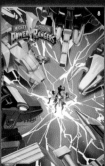

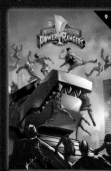